The
Whodunit
Detective Agency

The Gold Mystery

GROSSET & DUNLAP
Penguin Young Readers Group
An Imprint of Penguin Random House LLC

Penguin supports copyright. Copyright fuels creativity, encourages diverse voices, promotes free speech, and creates a vibrant culture. Thank you for buying an authorized edition of this book and for complying with copyright laws by not reproducing, scanning, or distributing any part of it in any form without permission. You are supporting writers and allowing Penguin to continue to publish books for every reader.

Original title: Guldmysteriet
Text by Martin Widmark
Original cover and illustrations by Helena Willis

English language edition copyright © 2016 Penguin Random House LLC.
Original edition published by Bonnier Carlsen Bokförlag, Sweden, 2004. Text
copyright © 2004 by Martin Widmark. Illustrations copyright © 2004 by Helena Willis.
Published in 2016 by Grosset & Dunlap, an imprint of Penguin Random House LLC,
345 Hudson Street, New York, New York 10014. GROSSET & DUNLAP is
a trademark of Penguin Random House LLC. Manufactured in China.

Library of Congress Cataloging-in-Publication Data is available.

ISBN 9780448480800   10 9 8 7 6 5 4 3 2 1

The Whodunit Detective Agency

The Gold Mystery

Martin Widmark
illustrated by **Helena Willis**

Grosset & Dunlap
An Imprint of Penguin Random House

MUSEUM STREET

Museum

M

PLEASANT VALLEY SCHO

News

Church

CHURCH STREET

Post Office

The Jeweler

HOT DOG

The Whodunit Detective
Agency Headquarters

The Gold Mystery

The books in *The Whodunit Detective Agency* series are set in the charming little town of Pleasant Valley. It's the sort of close-knit community where nearly everyone knows one another. The town and the characters are all fictional, of course . . . or are they?

The main characters, Jerry and Maya, are classmates and close friends who run a small detective agency together.

  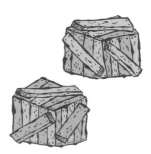

The people:

Maya

Jerry

Randolph Larson,
the police chief

Larry Mernard,
the bank manager

Roger Birchfield,
the head teller

Maria Gonzales de la Cruz,
the head of security

CHAPTER 1

Five Hundred and Fifty Pounds of Pure Gold

It was a beautiful, warm afternoon in July. School was out, and Maya and Jerry had nothing but free time. So far that summer they had spent a lot of time riding their bikes, looking for adventure. That morning they had set out on their bikes as usual. And now, they had joined the police chief on a dock in the harbor. They were watching a wooden crate as it was hoisted out of a big ship.

"Here comes the gold," said the police chief with excitement. "Five hundred and fifty pounds of solid gold!"

"I wonder how much it's worth," said Jerry.

"Let's see," said the police chief, pushing his cap to the back of his head. "Probably more like sixteen million dollars, I'd say."

"Wow," said Jerry, impressed.

"Why is all this gold coming to Pleasant Valley?" asked Maya.

"Well, it's not going to stay here," explained the police chief. "Tomorrow the gold heads to a big bank in another city. But tonight we are responsible for it."

"Where will the gold spend the night?" asked Jerry. "The hotel, like other visitors?"

"Very funny, Jerry," said Maya, rolling her eyes.

"We'll keep it in the safest place in Pleasant Valley," replied the police chief. "The bank vault, of course!"

The crate was loaded next to another similar-looking crate on the back of a truck. A dark-haired woman in uniform walked over. She saluted the police chief, who saluted her right back.

"Maria Gonzales de la Cruz," said the woman with a smile. "Head of security at the bank."

"Randolph Larson," replied the police chief. "It's a pleasure to meet you! Are you new at the bank? I don't think we've met before."

"That's right." The security officer smiled. "I've been at the bank for about three weeks. Now," she said, holding out a piece of paper, "I need your signature here."

"What's that you're signing?" Maya asked the police chief. She stood on tiptoe to see what was on the piece of paper. "Gold: five hundred and fifty pounds," she read. Maya couldn't see what else it said because the security officer's thumb was in the way.

"A consignment note," explained Maria Gonzales de la Cruz, smiling at Maya.

"It shows that we received the gold," explained the police chief, who signed the bottom.

The security officer tore off a yellow copy and gave it to the police chief, who folded the paper and tucked it in the pocket of his uniform.

"Okay, we're off to the bank," said Maria Gonzales de la Cruz as she jumped into the truck.

"Come on, kids," said the police chief, hopping onto his bike. "Let's head that way, too."

When Jerry, Maya, and the police chief reached Pleasant Valley's bank, the security officer was hard at work wheeling the second crate inside. A bald-headed man in a gray suit watched from a nearby spot. He looked worried.

"Careful there, Maria. Make sure it doesn't tip over," he said to the security officer.

"Do you need a hand?" asked the police chief.

The man in the gray suit looked up in surprise. Jerry thought he seemed pretty nervous.

I'd probably be jumpy, too, he thought. *That gold is worth a lot of money.*

"Thanks for the offer, but I've got this," said Maria to the police chief. After a few more grunts, she disappeared into the bank.

Maya rested her bike against the wall of the building and looked through the window

into the bank. She saw the security officer wheeling the crate into a big bank vault. Maya looked at her watch. It showed ten to six.

Then she saw Maria Gonzales pulling the heavy door to the vault closed.

"Well, well, the police chief is here to make sure everything goes smoothly," said the man in the gray suit.

He walked over to the police chief and held out his hand. The police chief and the man shook.

"This is the bank manager, Larry Mernard," said the police chief to Jerry and Maya.

Maya looked into the bank again. The security officer was now standing with her back to Maya and the others, adjusting something above the door to the vault. Maya leaned closer to the window but couldn't see exactly what Maria Gonzales was doing.

"It's a big day for our little bank here in Pleasant Valley," continued the police chief.

"And a stressful one," acknowledged the bank manager. "Just imagine if something were to go wrong!"

Larry Mernard wiped his forehead with a handkerchief.

Caramba, What Terrible Weather!

The police chief slapped the bank manager on the back.

"But what could possibly go wrong?" asked the police chief.

"Oh, well, nothing really," replied Larry Mernard. "We have all the equipment you need to keep gold safe: a bank vault and a security camera. But I still feel so nervous! Just imagine if something happened tonight!"

"The door to the vault looked pretty thick," said Maya encouragingly.

"Plus," added the bank manager, "there are a few more safety precautions. You have to have the right key and the right combination to open the door to the vault."

"And you're the only one who has the key and knows the combination?" asked the police chief.

"Exactly," answered the bank manager, patting his pocket, where a bunch of keys jingled.

Never one to miss an opportunity to learn about how to stop a thief, Jerry took out a notebook and pen from his pocket.

"Who works at the bank?" he asked.

"Is this an interrogation or what?" the bank manager said nervously.

The police chief smiled and pointed to Maya and Jerry.

"How silly of me! I forgot to introduce my two assistants, Jerry and Maya. They have helped me solve a lot of tricky cases."

"Nice to meet you," said the bank manager.

He straightened his tie and glanced uneasily into the bank. "Well, as I said, there are three of us on staff. I'm the manager, and Maria Gonzales de la Cruz is the head of security.

She's worked here for three weeks and is very efficient and careful."

"And strong," said the police chief admiringly. "Those crates weren't light—that's for sure!"

"Maria is from Spain," continued the bank manager. "She's always saying, '*Caramba*, what terrible weather,' even on a warm and sunny day like today."

"That's funny . . . ," said Maya with a laugh. "Anyway, you said there were three of you working here . . . ?"

"That's right. There's me and Maria— and then Roger Birchfield, of course," said the bank manager. "Roger is the head teller and keeps all the papers in order. He has worked here for many, many years. He's actually going to retire soon. He can't wait for the day, he said. He claims that all those numbers have turned him gray."

Jerry, Maya, and the police chief looked around but didn't see a third person, gray or otherwise.

The bank manager saw them looking and said quickly, "No, Roger isn't here right now. He . . . had to go to the doctor. He said he had a pain in his knee."

"Okay . . . ," said the police chief. "Anyway, you said something about a security camera?"

"That's right," said Larry Mernard. "It runs from six o'clock in the evening until eight o'clock in the morning—when I come in. During that time, everything that happens in the bank is filmed. And it's all recorded and kept on our computer. Nobody can approach the door to the vault without being caught on camera."

Maya looked at her watch again. "So . . . in four minutes the camera will start recording in the bank."

"It all sounds foolproof," said the police chief happily. "I should think you can sleep quite soundly tonight, Larry. Tomorrow the gold will head off, and it will be nice and quiet in your little bank again."

"I hope it will," the bank manager said with a sigh. Once again he took out his handkerchief and wiped his forehead.

The security officer, Maria Gonzales de la Cruz, came out of the bank.

"It's time to lock up now, sir," she said. "Two minutes until the camera starts rolling."

The bank manager, Larry Mernard, went into the bank. Maya looked through the window and saw him walk over to the vault.

"*Ay, caramba!* Señor Police Chief, what do you think of this weather?" cried the security officer.

The police chief squinted at the sun, which was still high in the sky, and replied, "Now that you mention it, it is pretty hot today."

Suddenly, Maria stamped her feet on the pavement with a loud bang. Then she straightened her back and snapped her fingers.

The police chief, Jerry, and Maya looked at her in surprise.

What on earth is she doing? wondered Maya.

"Flamenco!" shrieked Maria Gonzales de la Cruz and spun around and around toward the police chief. "The music and soul of Spain! Señor, you would make an excellent flamenco dancer!"

The security officer clicked her fingers around the police chief's head, and he blushed.

"Well, I'm not so sure," he said shyly. "I've never been a great one for dancing." The police chief gulped and went on, "I prefer wrestling . . . maybe I could show you a hold or two?"

But before the police chief had time to put the security officer in a wrestling hold, the bank manager came out of the bank.

"That's it, then," he said. "The gold is locked up, and the security camera is running. Now, let's all go home and keep our fingers crossed that nothing happens tonight."

The bank manager, Larry Mernard, and the security officer, Maria Gonzales de la Cruz, said good-bye and walked off along Commercial Road.

Jerry, Maya, and the police chief got on their bikes, and the police chief muttered, "*Caramba*, that's an interesting way to keep a bank secure!"

CHAPTER 3

The Gold Is Gone!

Early the next morning, Jerry and Maya cycled along at full speed toward the bank. The police chief had woken up Maya with a phone call. And of course she then called Jerry.

"The gold is gone!" the police chief informed her.

Maya and Jerry braked sharply outside the bank on Commercial Road and ran in through the open door. Inside the bank, the police chief was sitting at the counter, staring at a computer screen.

"What's happened?" asked Maya.

"The gold—it's gone." The police chief groaned.

"But how did *that* happen?" asked Jerry. "What about the vault? And the keys?"

The police chief shook his head and said, "I don't know. I've called the central police station and informed them of what's happened. This is very serious. But come and look at this!"

Jerry and Maya walked around the desk and looked over the police chief's shoulder. On the screen they could see the bank building.

"This is the film from the security camera," explained the police chief.

"Good," said Maya. "If the gold has been stolen, the thief must be on the recording from last night."

"That's what's strange," said the police chief. "I've looked through all of it, from six o'clock in the evening, when the recording started yesterday, all the way through until this morning when the camera switched off at eight."

"And . . . ?" asked Jerry.

"Nothing," said the police chief.

"What do you mean, nothing?" said Maya. "The gold can't have *vanished* out of the vault."

The police chief sighed again and continued, "I can't understand it. The vault is empty, the gold is gone, and the cameras haven't recorded a thing!"

"And where were the staff?" asked Jerry. "The bank manager, the head of security, and the head teller?"

The police chief took an envelope from the pocket of his uniform.

"See for yourselves," he said and handed the envelope to Maya. "This was on the floor in the vault."

Maya opened the envelope, took out the paper that was in it, and read it aloud.

We have taken the gold. The staff are our hostages. Do not follow us—because if you do . . . !

"The staff are hostages!" said Jerry when she had finished. "How awful!"

"And if we try to follow the thieves, they are threatening to hurt Larry, Maria, and Roger," said Maya.

"If the staff has been kidnapped, who discovered that the gold was gone?" asked Jerry.

"The man who owns the pet store along the street. He was walking past the bank just after eight o'clock this morning. He saw that the door was open but there were no lights on. He didn't dare go in himself so he called me immediately from his store. When I got here I discovered the vault was closed and the gold—gone!"

Jerry and Maya looked at the computer screen for a moment. The film showed the closed vault door. The police chief fast-forwarded and rewound the film several times but they couldn't spot anything out of the ordinary, and in the end he switched the screen off.

"Strange," said Jerry. "The door wasn't opened all night but all the gold has disappeared!"

"There must be another door in there," Maya said finally.

"Another door?" said the police chief in surprise. "What do you mean?"

"Well, if anyone had left with the gold through the front of the vault, they would have been filmed by the cameras, right?"

"Yes, that's true," replied the police chief.

"So the gold must have disappeared some other way. Come on, let's take a closer look at the bank vault."

Maya and the police chief went into the vault. Jerry waited at the counter. Next to the computer screen there was a red button. A small label next to the button said "camera." Jerry looked around the room and soon discovered the camera on the wall by the front door.

CAMERA

Jerry pressed the button, and the camera's red light immediately went on. He could see the inside of the bank on the screen.

Jerry took out his trademark notebook and pen. Then he started sketching the layout of the bank on a sheet of his notebook. He drew the vault and the counter where he sat. Finally he drew the camera on the wall.

Maya and the police chief were busily investigating the walls inside the vault. Next they examined the floor and the ceiling.

They knocked and banged to see if they could possibly find a concealed door or a hole where the gold could have been smuggled out.

Maya saw a rolled-up piece of gray fabric on top of a tall steel cabinet, but other than that—nothing.

In the middle of the floor were the two wooden crates that Maria Gonzales de la Cruz, the head of security, had wheeled in

the previous day. Maya and the police chief lifted the lids of the crates to see if they were empty. They were. The police chief and Maya each jumped up and sat on a crate.

"This is a mystery," said the police chief. "How in the world did the gold get out of a locked vault monitored by a security camera?"

Maya thought back to the previous day. It started at the harbor . . . they watched the crates leave the ship . . . they met the head of security . . . the police chief signed the consignment note . . .

"Do you still have that consignment note?" asked Maya, pointing to the police chief's pocket.

The police chief looked surprised but then felt in his pocket and nodded. He handed the piece of paper to her.

Maya took the yellow copy of the consignment note and read out loud:

"'Type of goods: gold. Weight: five hundred and fifty pounds. Number of packages: one. Signature: Randolph Larson.'"

Five hundred and fifty pounds of gold, thought Maya, *worth more than sixteen million dollars—gone.* And to think: The gold was only supposed to stay in Pleasant Valley one night.

But then she realized something and looked at the consignment note again. "Listen to this! 'Number of packages: one.' That means *one* crate! There are *too many* crates in here!" she shouted.

SHIPPING BILL 131

ARRIVAL DATE: 7/12

ARRIVAL CITY: Pleasant Valley

FURTHER TRANSPORT: 7/13

TYPE OF GOODS: gold

WEIGHT: 550 lbs

NUMBER OF PACKAGES: 1

NAME: SIGNATURE OF CONSIGNEE: R. Larson

DATE: 7/12

CHAPTER 4

Wave to the Camera!

The police chief looked at Maya and sighed.

"I know!" he said.

"What? You knew that?" said Maya with surprise.

"Yes, of course. *Neither* of these crates should be here," he replied crossly. "Both of them are supposed to be on the train by now. Two crates on a train, full of gold."

Maya passed the consignment note to the police chief and asked him to read it carefully. And when the police chief had read it himself, he finally understood what Maya was talking about.

"So one of these crates shouldn't be here!" said Maya, pointing to the crates they were sitting on.

"But why go to so much trouble to wheel in *two* big crates, if only one of them contains gold?" asked the police chief.

"Probably because the other crate contained something very important," replied Maya.

"And what could that be?" asked the police chief.

"No idea," said Maya, "but I think it has something to do with the disappearance of the gold."

She and the police chief took a closer look at the two crates. They opened them. The police chief looked in one, and Maya looked in the other.

"This one's completely empty," said the police chief.

"This one is, too," said Maya, "but on closer inspection . . ."

Maya leaned farther into the crate. She had spotted something in the corner. A hair.

A short gray curly hair. Maya passed it to the police chief.

"It could be from someone who packed the gold into the crate before it even got to Pleasant Valley," said the police chief.

"Neither the bank manager nor the security officer have hair like this."

"True," said Maya, "and the head teller, Roger Birchfield, wasn't even here. He went to the doctor yesterday."

Maya and the police chief closed the crates and left the vault.

Jerry had now drawn the entire inside of the bank, and he could see on the screen when Maya and the police chief came out of the vault.

"Wave at the camera, Maya," joked Jerry.

"Where is it?" asked Maya.

"There, above the front door," said Jerry, pointing.

Maya stood in the doorway to the vault and waved to the camera. Jerry could see her on the computer screen. But . . . he could only see *part* of Maya. When she waved to him, her right arm disappeared from the screen.

Jerry looked up at the camera on the wall. Was it set up wrong?

"Stay there," called Jerry. On his sketch, he drew in the part of the door that the camera covered.

"What are you doing?" called Maya.

The police chief walked over to Jerry and looked at what he had written on the paper.

"Now walk forward in a zigzag toward the main door," Jerry said to Maya as he stared at the screen intently.

Maya wondered what Jerry was up to, but she followed his instructions. Jerry watched her on the screen, all the while sketching in where she could be seen and where she disappeared from the picture.

"Good heavens," muttered the police chief from behind Jerry. "It looks as if . . ."

"I'm here!" called Maya from the outer door. "Would you like me to dance a bit for you, too? How about the flamenco?"

Maya stamped on the floor.

"Maya, come look at this!" said Jerry.

On his sketch, Jerry had drawn in the exact parts of the bank the camera covered.

"Look!" he said. "The spots where the camera misses form an invisible corridor, from one side of the vault door, along the wall here, right out to the main door. The thieves could have walked along there without the camera seeing them."

"Well done, Jerry!" said Maya.

"That means someone could have adjusted the camera deliberately," said the police chief as he scratched his head.

There were three chairs by the front door for customers who were waiting in the bank. The police chief walked up to them, took a chair, and placed it under the camera.

He was just about to stand on it to

examine the camera a little more closely when he stopped. "Look at this, kids," he said, pointing to the seat of the chair.

Maya and Jerry walked over to the police chief and looked at the chair. There were two clear footprints on the green fabric of the seat.

"I think we are on the right track," said the police chief, nodding.

CHAPTER 5

Lukewarm Drinks

The police chief, Jerry, and Maya walked out onto the street in front of the bank. The sun was shining in a clear blue sky, and it looked like it would be at least as hot as the day before.

"Come on, kids," said the police chief. "Let's go and sit in the shade under the tree over there."

The police chief pointed to a tree on the other side of Commercial Road.

"I'll go get us each a drink," said Jerry, and he headed toward the supermarket on the other side of the street.

"Get really cold ones," called the police chief.

Maya and the police chief sat down on the grass under the tree.

The police chief loosened his tie a little and said, "Let's go over what we know."

"We know that gold worth more than sixteen million dollars was stolen from the bank last night," Maya began.

"And what else?" asked the police chief.

"That someone had moved the security camera, and that there is one crate too many in the vault."

"And even if we knew who had taken the gold, we wouldn't dare to follow them . . ."

What we Know ① ② ❸ ④

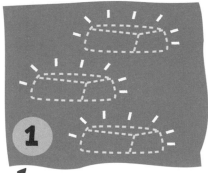

MORE THAN $16 MILLION IN GOLD STOLEN

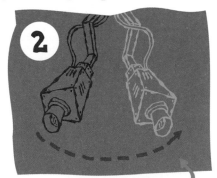

SOMEONE HAS TURNED THE CAMERA

". . . because the thieves have threatened to harm their hostages," Maya completed the sentence. "But the strange thing is . . . ," she went on.

"What?" asked the police chief.

". . . that the door wasn't opened all night. Even if the security camera was moved a bit, you can see on the film from the camera that the door was never opened."

"And yet the gold disappeared," said the police chief as he waved at Jerry, who was coming out of the supermarket.

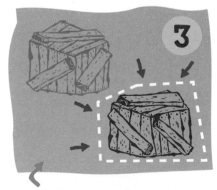

AN EXTRA CRATE IN THE BANK VAULT

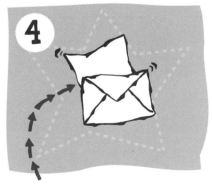

A RANSOM NOTE FROM THE ROBBERS

Jerry started walking across the street. He had three bottles in his hands. But suddenly he stopped—right in the middle of Commercial Road! A driver honked angrily, and Jerry jumped out of the way.

"What are you doing, Jerry?" asked Maya when he reached the tree. "Do you have sunstroke?"

"I just thought of something . . . ," said Jerry slowly.

He gave Maya and the police chief each a drink.

The police chief immediately opened his and put the bottle to his mouth.

He took a few deep swigs and then said, "Delicious, but it's not very cold!"

"No, exactly," said Jerry. "Lukewarm drinks . . . Maybe that's a clue . . ."

The police chief and Maya looked at Jerry.

"What do you mean?" asked the police chief. "What connection could there be between lukewarm drinks and five hundred and fifty pounds of lost gold?"

"I felt the bottles in the fridge in the store," explained Jerry. "They were all equally warm. So I asked one of the shop employees whether they had any cold ones. She told me that the refrigerator had broken down during the night."

"I still don't understand what this has to do with the missing gold," said Maya.

"Me neither," said the police chief, after he had drunk the last drops from his bottle.

"Just listen, it does," continued Jerry. "The employee apologized for not having any cold drinks, but said that the refrigerator had broken down *during the night,* and they don't work at night."

"Of course they don't," said Maya, who still couldn't understand what Jerry was getting at.

"So then I thought that it's actually quite unusual for people to work at night," said Jerry.

"In hospitals of course, or perhaps the fire station, but never at a . . ."

Then Maya understood! She jumped up and shouted.

"Aha! You're a genius, Jerry! Now I bet I know who stole the gold."

"You do?" asked the police chief in astonishment. "Do you know who it was, too, Jerry?"

Jerry nodded and said, "I think so."

CHAPTER 6

The Man in the Crate

The police chief looked at Jerry and Maya in amazement.

"I don't understand," he said. "How can you two know who stole the gold? All we've done is sit here under the tree and think a bit."

"Can I see the piece of paper the thieves left behind?" asked Jerry.

The police chief took the paper out of his pocket. Jerry read aloud:

"We have taken the gold. The staff are our hostages. Do not follow us—because if you do . . . !"

"What?" asked the chief.

"Not *what*," said Jerry. "The question is *when*."

"What do you mean, *when?*" asked the police chief.

"*When* did the thieves take the staff hostage?" continued Jerry.

The police chief was silent for a long moment, then he finally understood.

"What nerve! Of course Larry and the rest of the staff weren't working in the bank at night! They haven't been taken hostage at all!"

Jerry and Maya looked at each other and smiled broadly.

"We even saw the bank manager and the head of security leave the bank ourselves, just after six," said Maya. "*When* could they have been taken hostage?"

"But we didn't see the head teller at all," said the police chief. "He was at the doctor. But wait a minute! Maybe we should check that!"

The police chief took his phone out of his pocket and keyed in a number.

After exchanging a few words, he put the phone back in his pocket.

"Roger Birchfield was *not* at the doctor yesterday," said the police chief.

"If I have guessed right, he was much closer to us than we thought," said Maya.

"Where then?" asked the police chief. "What do you mean?"

"I'm beginning to think," said Jerry, "that the gold was stolen by the three employees at the bank. The bank manager, Larry Mernard; the head of security, Maria Gonzales de la Cruz; and the head teller, Roger Birchfield. They planned the whole thing and carried it out together."

"The head teller was in the second crate!" said Maya. "That hair we found must be one of his. It was gray and came from an older person. Remember what Larry told us? Roger is due to retire soon."

"Exactly," said Jerry. "He keeps complaining that all those numbers have made him go gray."

"So that was why the bank manager was so nervous when Maria Gonzales was wheeling the crates into the vault!" said the police chief. "Roger Birchfield was hidden inside one of the crates! And to think Larry had us believe he was worried about the bank protecting the gold. What a liar! Okay, snack break is over, kids! Time to get back to work!"

Jerry, Maya, and the police chief got up from the grass. The police chief took out his phone again.

"I'll call the central police station," he said. "Now that we know who we're actually looking for."

The police chief called and described the three suspects. Then he put his phone away and rubbed his hands.

"They'll soon be caught, you'll see!" he said with satisfaction. "The long arm of the law can be very long, indeed." He chuckled.

But Jerry and Maya looked at each another doubtfully. There were still too many pieces of the puzzle missing.

"There's one thing I still don't understand," said Maya. "Why did they write that they'd been taken hostage?"

"So that we wouldn't pursue them, of course," said the police chief. "They wanted to get as far away as possible with all that gold before the hunt began."

"Yes, but they must have realized that we would discover their scheme," said Jerry. "We know they don't work in the bank at night."

"They probably thought that the theft— and their fake note—would be discovered much later in the day," said Maya. "If so, we would have thought they'd been taken hostage this morning. But thanks to the man from the pet store, we realized that the gold had disappeared during the night."

Jerry nodded. He, Maya, and the police chief started walking back toward the bank.

CHAPTER 7

Ready to Roll!

When they reached the bank again, the police chief stopped inside the door.

"But," he said, "we still don't know how the gold got out through the closed door of the vault!"

Jerry had taken out his notepad and was looking at the sketch of the bank he had made earlier. Then he tore tiny little pieces of paper off the pad. He placed them on the floor so that they showed precisely which parts of the bank the security camera recorded during the night.

"Let's try to reconstruct the crime," he said.

"What?" asked Maya.

"We'll reenact the crime," said Jerry, "to see how the thieves did it. Maya, you be the head teller hiding in the vault. Pull the door shut from the inside so that everything is like it was last night."

"What about me?" asked the police chief.

"You check the screen to see if I manage to keep out of the picture," said Jerry. "I am the bank manager," he continued. "And I am going to try to creep along the wall and open the vault door without being seen on the screen."

The police chief walked around the counter and pressed the button which started the camera over the main door. Maya went into the vault and carefully pulled the heavy vault door partially closed.

"Be careful, Maya," Jerry called out to her. "Make sure you don't let the door shut all the way. If it does, you'll be stuck in there until we find the bank manager, arrest him, and get the keys to unlock the door."

"Okay," said Maya from inside the vault. She left the door open just enough to see through.

"Ready to roll!" said the police chief.

Jerry stood under the camera by the outer door.

"Can you see me now?" he asked.

The police chief looked at the screen and said, "No."

Jerry moved toward the vault door, hugging the wall. He was careful to keep himself between the wall and the pieces of paper on the floor.

BANK DIRECTOR
MAX SMART

"Still can't see you!" called the police chief.

Maya looked out through the crack in the door and saw Jerry creeping along the wall, getting closer and closer to the vault door. She saw him reach out his hand and pretend to unlock the door.

"There! I can see you!" called the police chief suddenly.

Jerry pulled his hand back and dropped

to the floor. He crawled toward the keyhole.

"I can see you again!" shouted the police chief behind the counter.

Jerry stood up and shook his head. "It's impossible to get to the keyhole without being seen." He sighed. "I don't understand it! How in the world did they get the gold out?"

Inside the vault, Maya examined the two empty crates in the middle of the floor.

How nerve-wracking, she thought, *to sit in that crate, just waiting to steal the gold.*

Maya looked around the vault. Then she caught sight of the length of gray fabric she had seen earlier, lying rolled up on top of the tall cabinet.

Maya pulled out one of the drawers in the cabinet and climbed up. She reached for the roll of fabric and just barely got hold of it. She held on to the end of the roll and pulled the fabric down.

Her eyes widened when she realized what

she was holding! They had already figured out *when* and *who,* and now she understood *how* the theft had been carried out!

"Jerry! Chief Larson!" she cried. "I figured it out! I know how they stole the gold!"

In her excitement about the discovery, Maya took a step backward on the drawer . . . and missed the edge of it. She lost her balance and toppled over! Maya stretched out her hands to stop herself and . . .

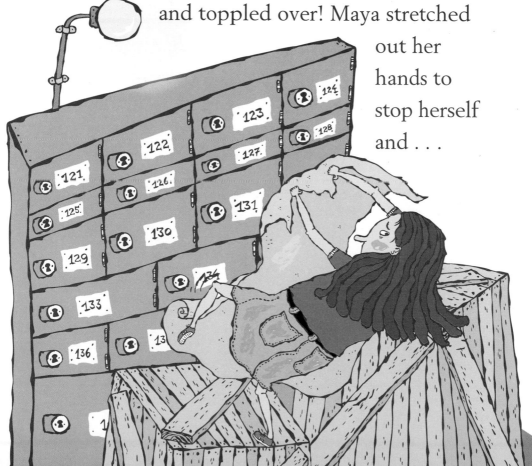

pushed the vault door completely shut with a loud *click!*

"Maya!" shouted Jerry as he saw the door to the vault shut.

"Oh dear! Not the vault door!" cried the police chief.

He rushed to the door and struggled to open it.

"Now we *have* to find the manager! He is the only one who has the keys!" said Jerry.

"What was that Maya said just before the door shut?" asked the police chief.

"That she knew how they did it. Maya figured out how they stole the gold," answered Jerry with a sigh.

CHAPTER 8

What a Clever Kid!

"**M**aya," called Jerry as loudly as he could, but he could only hear a muffled reply from inside the vault.

"The door is too thick." The police chief sighed.

"Poor Maya," said Jerry. "I'd hate to be trapped in there!"

"Let's try to get hold of a locksmith," said the police chief. "Not that I think . . ."

The police chief's dismal thought was interrupted by a loud honking outside. Jerry and the police chief ran to the windows to see what it was.

Outside they saw a tow truck, which was towing a black car.

Behind it was a police car. Jerry and the police chief went outside to see what was going on.

A young policeman jumped out of the police car and saluted.

"Police Chief Randolph Larson?" asked the young policeman.

"That is correct," said the police chief as he raised his hand in a return salute.

"I've heard a lot about you," said the other policeman.

"Well, well, that's nice. What brings you to Pleasant Valley?"

"I've got some people in the police car that I think you are anxious to see," said the young policeman, gesturing to the backseat of his car with his thumb.

The police chief and Jerry leaned forward and looked into the police car. And there they saw the head of security, Maria Gonzales de la Cruz; the bank manager, Larry Mernard; and a man with curly gray hair who was probably the head teller, Roger Birchfield.

All three looked very angry. And all three wore a new pair of handcuffs.

"We found them on the highway.

Their back tire had gotten a flat. And when we drove past them, we saw that they were piling up gold bars by the side of the road."

"What?" exclaimed Jerry. "Why would they unload all that gold where anyone could see them?"

"They had to," explained the policeman. "The spare tire was at the bottom of the trunk."

"Fantastic!" said the police chief. "But if you'll excuse me, I have to ask you to let me borrow them for a moment."

The police chief opened the door to the back of the car and helped the thieves climb out.

"The gold is still in the trunk of the car," said the young policeman. "Shall we start carrying it in again?"

"We have to unlock the vault first," replied the police chief, and he put his hand in the bank manager's jacket pocket.

He took out a bundle of keys and hurried into the bank. The police chief tried a few keys before he found the right one. The door to the bank vault opened, and Maya came running out with the piece of gray fabric.

"I know how they did it!" she yelled. "Look at this!"

Maya was so excited that she didn't notice that they were no longer alone in the bank.

"They hung this gray fabric in front of the vault door."

The police chief and Jerry gasped, because once opened, the fabric looked just like the vault door. Someone had painted it to match the real door.

"Look at this!" Maya said. "The tacks that held the painting of the vault door are still in the door frame above the actual vault door. The real door was never locked," she said. "And the film from the security camera didn't show any difference between the piece of fabric and the real door!"

"*Caramba!* What a clever kid!" said Maria Gonzales de la Cruz, impressed.

Maya turned around quickly and looked in surprise at the security officer and the other two thieves.

"*That* was what you were doing when I looked into the bank when the gold arrived," Maya said.

"But then the bank manager went in and locked up," said the police chief.

"We never saw—how could we?" Jerry said. "We had a private flamenco performance outside on the pavement. Remember all that finger snapping, Chief? And we didn't see him pull out a chair and twist the camera above the door either. The only

This is what happened:

1. BANK VAULT
2. CRATE WITH GOLD
3. CRATE WITH TELLER
4. BANK VAULT DOOR
5. FABRIC DOOR
6. BANK BUILDING
7. CASHIER
8. CAMERA
9. FRONT DOOR
10. CAR

thing we saw were his footprints on the chair."

Jerry pointed at the manager's feet.

"Right," said the police chief slowly. "Now, let's see if I've understood the entire thing . . . This is a pretty tricky case."

The police chief took a deep breath and started talking. "A few minutes before six, two crates arrive at the bank. The head of security wheels them into the vault. One contains five hundred and fifty pounds of pure gold. And the head teller is hidden in the other one. The security officer hangs up that piece of fabric and then goes out to the manager on the street."

He cleared his throat and continued. "The bank manager goes in and *pretends* to lock the vault door, and before he leaves the premises, he adjusts the camera so that it only films half of the door. At night the bank manager and the security officer come back here and the head teller has climbed out of his crate inside the vault. But I don't understand . . . surely the camera would have filmed anyone coming out of the vault?"

"I would imagine that the cashier was kneeling down behind the fabric door and pushing out one gold bar after another under the side of the fabric that the camera was *not* monitoring, don't you think?" said Jerry as he looked at Roger Birchfield, the head teller.

The head teller nodded and looked down at the floor.

"And on the other side of the fabric, beyond the angle of the camera, stood the security officer and the bank manager, receiving the bars and carrying them out to the waiting car," continued Jerry. "And when the clock struck eight this morning and the camera switched off, Roger was able to take down the fabric, roll it up, and leave the vault."

"But before you left, you wrote a note

that said you'd been captured and held hostage," said the police chief, wagging his finger at the three thieves. "That was a really mean trick. We were worried about you!"

Finally, when all the gold bars were back in the vault, the police chief locked up with the manager's key and said, "Now it's time to take a little walk to our lockup!"

Jerry and Maya remained outside the bank for a while, watching the police chief lead the gold thieves away.

"Just imagine how close they came to getting away with the gold," said Jerry.

"And what would have happened to me *then*?" said Maya uneasily, and she shivered in spite of the heat.

"There are risks attached to being a detective," said Jerry in a serious tone. "But let's go for a swim now, shall we?"

"Okay," said Maya. "I'd love to cool down after all this."

And the next day everyone in Pleasant Valley read in the newspaper about what had happened at the bank on one hot July day:

GOLD ON THE LOOSE
RECOVERED

Once again the young detectives Jerry and Maya have helped justice fight crime. This time, 550 pounds of pure gold vanished from the bank. To make matters worse, it was believed that the bank staff had been taken hostage.

"This was an especially serious case," explained the police chief to the *Pleasant Valley Gazette*. "But thanks to a lot of cunning, a lukewarm drink, and an overloaded car, my assistant detectives and I caught the thieves!"